Life Is A Movie

A game of life you can't play twice.

By
Fatima Sidibe

Hello readers. This captivating book will continuously include different combined short stories to make an outstanding collection. The author will be releasing new and interesting parts of the series on a monthly basis through interesting and captivating narratives that are worth reading. Readers should expect captivating stories that are consistent and well-formulated and worth sparing reading time.

By using the technique of the series, the author will organize the scenes in a simplified manner and make it easy to follow, and get the book flow with ease. You are welcome to explore and learn new experiences from this critically designed book series.

Enjoy!

ACKNOWLEDGMENTS

To begin with I would like to thank God for all of my blessings. I would like to thank my mom, Dawn. Thank you for always being there. To my son, Daquan, I love you dearly. Special thanks to my sister, Dominique. Tanayja, my best friend, thank you for being so supportive. Mr. Jones, thank you for believing in me. To my father, Adam, thank you for being the man you are.

Aunt Vivian, I miss you so much and wish you were here to witness this moment with me.

Many thanks to all my family and friends, without your support this wouldn't have been possible.

CONTENTS

HOW IT STARTED

Knock knock was all Cheyenne heard while at the kitchen table studying for her GED. Boom. Boom. The noise was closer and louder at the front door. "What the hell is going on?"

Yelled Latoya from the master bedroom. "Who is that banging on the door?"

Cheyenne said, "I don't know. I didn't expect anyone. I'm just trying to study for my exam next month." With no sign of fear or anxiety, Latoya opened the door, and it was Stephanie Chey, best friend.

Latoya was Cheyenne's older sister, with them being four years apart. Their parents were killed in a car accident when Cheyenne was only six months old. Their Aunt Lee raised them until she died from diabetes. By then Latoya had been twenty-one, and Chey was seventeen.

"Someone has been shot in Tyrell's building!" Stephanie was shouting as soon as the door opened.

"What?" Chey said, shocked. She instantly dropped her pen, barely able to talk. She reached for her phone and saw four missed calls, but they were all from Stephanie.

Chey glanced down at her belly and prayed that it wasn't Tyrell. He was always outside when they were apart. He also sold drugs, so you know how that went. But he was the father of her unborn child. He lived on Main Street, which was about five minutes away from her.

Cheyenne quickly jumped over the coffee table, tripping on her nephew's yellow ducky toy, and rushed to her room to get dressed. She put on a black Victoria's Secret sweat suit with pink-in-white lettering on her chest and going down her right leg. She grabbed her black Moncler coat and was out the door.

Stephanie was right behind her. Toya could not come because her son Darren, who was just four years old and sick, was unable to make it.

It was mid-December, nearly 11 p.m. Chey and Steph took a taxi to Main Street. Chey could not help but think: what if she were confronted with something she was not prepared for? She felt something was wrong in her heart, like women's intuition. She could not tell if it was her stomach pounding or the baby moving.

"We must stop at the corner. The taxi driver stated it cost seven dollars, even though it was only four blocks away.

This was the minimum amount they could travel anywhere. If they went one more block, it would have cost them ten dollars. Cheyenne reached into her pocket but realized that she didn't have her wallet. She had nothing in her pockets; all she could feel was the little hole at the bottom.

Stephanie stated, "I got it," while handing a twenty-dollar bill to the taxi driver.

Stephanie was wide-eyed as she got out of the taxi. There was a helicopter and about ten police cars. There was yellow caution tape everywhere, and there were a lot of people recording their phone conversations.

Cheyenne ran to the officers. "Please, I am eight months pregnant and just want to make sure that my child's father is okay."

"Do you live on the same block as your child's father, ma'am?" Do you have identification?

Cheyenne couldn't stand straight because of all the confusion and noise. She was looking and searching for Tyrell, his mom or sister, at least, as hard as she could with her eyes, but she didn't see anyone.

Stephanie was talking with the men in the street who were also being nosy. But she had a reason: her unborn goddaughter's dad could be killed or shot at this point.

"Miss, it's late. The officer advised that if you don't reside on this block, you should call him at home.

There was a shooting in building 271, and the shooter was nearby. That was Tyrell's building. That was all Chey needed to hear. She went to find Steph but before she could even take one step, she passed out, luckily, the officers were within arm's reach to catch her.

As Stephanie ran across the street towards Cheyenne, the crowd was running towards her as well. As she approached Chey, she saw a puddle of water with the slightest pink color to it. It was just too much for one night.

The officer called dispatch. "We need an ambulance at the corner of 279 Main Street. A pregnant woman between the age of seventeen and twenty-one passed out and we think her water broke."

In less than five minutes, the ambulance arrived. Stephanie called Toya, using her watch to find out which hospital Chey was being taken to. Chey passed out on Main Street. They're taking her to St. Mary's Hospital. I'll call you at the hospital about the rest.

After Aunt Lee died, Tyrell and Cheyenne became closer. Tyrell was a popular and handsome boy in the hood. Although they used to be close friends, Chey started to smoke more marijuana than usual. He loved it all the time, and she saw him more often. He was always attracted to her, but he also knew her worth and didn't want to hurt her feelings.

He had told her, "You're too beautiful to be smoking," when he brought her some marijuana one day

"Yeah, I know. "I don't want my lips turning black, but right now, I'm stressed."

He replied, "Why?"

"My aunt died two weeks ago, and I feel so alone without her. "I can still hear her voice inside my head." Tyrell stood at the top of the stairs while she was at the door. He just wanted to hug Chey because he found her attractive and felt her pain. At the age of 8, he lost his father, leaving him and his sister.

"Can you have company?" He asked Chey while gazing up at her. He pictured Chey taking off her tank top without a bra and kissing her neck towards her nipples. She hesitated but realized she wasn't ready to be alone, so she decided why not.

"Yes, I can have company. My sister is crazy cool."

Tyrell wore a red Ralph Lauren sweat suit with wheat colored construction boots. His hairline was always sharp. He was brown skin and about 6'1 and lord knows Chey loves her, a tall man.

"You can sit over there. "She pointed to the brown leather sectional couches. "Are you thirsty?" she asked him.

He replied, "Nah, I'm good. But we can order food because you're going to be hungry after we smoke."

She laughed and said, "You asked if you could smoke with me. Now you want to eat too."

"I just want to make sure you are good, that's all."

She was sure he meant no harm, so she reached for her phone to suggest Papa John's. They both agreed and shortly after they started watching Set It Off while they smoked. He was ready to leave before the food even came and the movie wasn't nearly finished yet. She wasn't sure if he was *ready* to leave or if he *had* to because his phone must have rung about 20 times. She walked him to the door, and he gave her a hug and some more marijuana and said,

"Don't smoke your life away, but it will help you for the moment."

She thanked him and closed the door behind him. She was blushing, and in that short time, she was unsure whether she was vulnerable, or if she'd indeed seen a new aspect of Tyrell that she'd never seen before.

CHEYENNE

"Miss, Miss can you hear me? Can you tell me your name?" nurse Joan asked.

"Chey, Cheyenne Brown," she responded. She was feeling dehydrated and was unsure of what had brought her to the hospital. The cry of a baby and the beeping of the electrocardiographic heart monitor woke her up.

"You are four centimeters dilated and your baby's heart rate has dropped to low, therefore you're likely to require an emergency C-section," Nurse Joan informed Chey.

"No," she said before the nurse could complete her sentence. "Can you please inform my friend to come over?" Stephanie started walking toward them before Nurse Joan could inform her.

"She won't be allowed to enter the room during the surgery and no one else will."

"How do you feel? Toya is on her way now but she is waiting for Dontae to come pick up Darren," Stephanie asked Chey

"Where is Tyrell?" she asked immediately

Before Steph could respond they were distracted by the sound of running and a rushing noise. There were about six doctors running down the hallway as if someone died, surprisingly they were running to them. A young, black, bald head doctor said to Chey

"Hi, my name is Dr. Williams and I will be the one that delivers your baby."

"Miss, do you want to sit in the waiting area? The friend you have in our care is safe," he said to Steph. He, along with the rest of the medical team, began pushing Chey toward the elevator. Everything was moving so fast.

"Dr. Williams, I need to call my child's father and I don't want to have a C-section," Chey said rudely. But who can blame her, a lot had happened. He started to slow down the gurney but was still pushing her slowly.

"Ms. Brown I understand that you are scared but your baby's heart rate is dropping as we speak and is at high risk. If we wait any longer you will be at risk as well."

She just looked at him and didn't say anything. The thought of it was terrifying. However, she didn't think about it. Not that she didn't care about her or the baby being at risk, but she was afraid to undergo surgery. *How did I get in this situation in the first place?* She thought to herself.

In the room where the operation was taking place, she was in a state of panic. Dr. Williams went to whisper something to the female nurse's ear. She quickly went out of the room once Dr. Williams was finished. The remainder of the staff was getting ready for the surgery. Dr. Williams walked over to Chey and told her he planned to allow Stephanie into the room. She was thrilled, even though it was not Tyrell, but it was better than having to be alone.

"Here is a little something that will make you drowsy, " he said while putting on a face mask while his assistant gave her a needle in her right arm.

"Count to ten Ms. Brown," his assistant asked "1,2,3,4. "

———

Chey woke up to Toya and Stephanie in her room. She was sleeping on a queen size bed with a 20-inch television on the wall.

Stephanie was on the recliner chair sleeping while Toya was sitting in the chair on her phone watching a movie. It was 5:53 am and the curtains were down so it was somewhat dim in the room.

"Good morning girl. Congratulations," Toya said as she looked up and saw that Chey was up.

"Good morning. Thank You girl, where is she? Where is Tyrell?"

"She is in the nursery, a big baby girl. 8 lbs 15 oz.

Tyrell's phone was off all night. I'm not sure."

"What do you mean? Where's my phone? You have my phone?"

Chey was shaking. She attempted to reach upwards, but the discomfort caught her off guard, pushing her back. The wrap around her stomach from the C-section was so tight. She could barely sit up or turn her body around. The surgery was among her most painful experiences, even though she could barely remember it from the anesthesia.

"Please leave your message for 911-911-9111," Tyrell's voicemail said. She hung up and called his mother's cell phone and her phone was off as well.

"What is happening?" As Chey screamed in annoyance,

Stephanie woke up

"Who got shot on Main Street?" She asked Stephanie immediately, before she could even say congratulations.

"Some dude name Rich...Tyesha's boyfriend." "Tyesha from Tyrell's building?" Chey asked surprisingly

"Yea."

"So why the fuck is Tyrell not answering then?" Toya was quiet, and her mouth was closed, and she was confused about why Stephanie didn't inform her about this earlier. She decided to call his older sister Diamond.

"Hi Diamond, how are you? Did you hear from your brother?"

"Hey Chey, no I haven't spoken to my brother, but he is fine you should not worry."

"There was a shooting on your block. I think in your building, and I haven't heard from him since."

"I spoke with my mom after the shooting and he is fine. Are you walking so you can go into labor?"

"I had your niece last night." Click

Chey hung up the phone in dismay because Diamond did not sound concerned about her brother. How can she just change the subject like that? She was sure of something, and the fact that she had just had a baby was more traumatic as she was hurting and anxious to find out what the hell was happening.

Diamond called Chey back. However, she redirected her to a voicemail. Chey's cell phone then informed Chey of a text message.

Congratulations Chey and I am sorry that you had to go through this alone. What hospital are you in, I will be up there later? Can't wait till I meet my niece!!!!

Diamond and Tyrell were just 11 months apart and were very close. If anyone knew where Tyrell was, that would be her. Diamond was aware she had a brother who was an excellent father, and would not miss the delivery in any way. So, what's the real reason?

She began to not pay attention to the text message, but then she realized that whatever it was that she couldn't possibly communicate with her on the phone. She, as well as Tyrell, believe that the police are listening to phone calls. Therefore, she decided to send her a text back, providing her with information on the hospital as well as giving her the food items she should bring to the hospital. If anyone was familiar with Chey, she was a girl who was a foodie. After the hassle of trying to determine the mystery surrounding Tyrell, she wants to meet her daughter. Due to the stress and chaos of everything that was happening, it was hard for her to even take in being a mother to her child.

"Can the nurse come? Can someone help me get an accessible wheelchair and transport me to the nursery? " Chey shouted out loudly, without noticing who she was asking.

Stephanie approached her and grasped her hand to help her get up. She was screaming in pain and tried to get up with ease. She tried moving her body towards the side and then sliding down, but it did not work. She was unable to reach the position that would allow her to lift herself off the bed without feeling discomfort. This was the first occasion she wanted to have a twin sized bed. She thought she could have climbed off of the bed more quickly or that it could be much easier.

"I cannot get up and walk again. It hurts so badly." "If it was some dick, you would have been up already." Stephanie's mouth was very sour! Toya and Chey began to laugh. However, you could see Chey was hurting. She couldn't even smile properly!

"I felt as if my stomach was going to explode. I'm unable to take a deep breath without hurting. "

"Let's try to assist her once more so that she will be able to see her big newborn baby." Toya mentioned

Toya tried to hold her hand as she scooted up slowly, but she was unable to endure the discomfort. At this point, it was evident that some wanted to quit, but the idea of seeing her daughter was more compelling. After trying different ways to get her out of bed and into the wheelchair, they had to accept that she couldn't bear the pain.

"Call for the nurse." Chey asked. After a few minutes, the nurse is in the room with an ER doctor.

"My name is Dr. Miller. How are you doing?" I'm sure you're suffering from pain. The nurse here can provide you with some painkillers while you wait. I'd like to keep in touch with you regarding your baby girl. She's doing well. We'd like to continue to check her heart rate till you are discharged, as it dropped to a low-level during labor. She will be connected to the machines 24/7 in the ICU. "

"So, my daughter won't be able to enter my bedroom?" Chey replied.

"No" She will remain in the ICU to allow us to monitor her.

You can visit her at any time. "

"I am in such discomfort that it's difficult to get up." "I am still sleeping on an old bed pan," she moaned with a sigh of frustration. She was upset, devastated, sad, lonely, whatever you think of that has to do with depression. This was her.

I am so sorry to hear that. The nurse will prescribe painkillers, and you'll need to take a nap. Your baby is in good hands, and in the event that anything changes, I'll be the first person to inform you. Sorry for the inconvenience that I'm not able to see you. "I've got other patients I need to check for," he said as he moved towards the front door. The nurse left the room with the doctor. Miller returned less than two minutes later with two Tylenol tablets.

"Thank you for staying up here with me, but you two should go home now and get some rest. I know your breath stinks Steph...shit your whole body probably stinks," Chey said looking at Stephanie and Toya.

"Fuck you." Steph said laughing at the same time as Toya. Chey, not realizing she could not be laughing, shouted in a loud, rapid blast. She was afraid she was about to burst once more.

"You aren't lying about that because I can use a shower myself."

"Do you want us to get you some breakfast before we go?" Toya asked while she fixed her clothes, getting ready to get dressed.

"No, I'm fine. I'm just trying to get to bed since I'm unable to do anything other than that."

The blanket was draped over her face, and she shut her eyes. Stephanie pulled out her black Mackage coat, and Toya put on her black and yellow Nuptse North Face. It was cold out there!

"Later girl and get some rest, we love you and will be back up here later." Toya said as she and Stephanie left the room.

<hr />

"WAKE UP BITCH" Diamond said. Diamond had brown skin and almost the same complexion as Tyrell. She also had hazel eyes, which would make her a perfect model. Although her hair was slicked back like a bob, it was long enough to be cute. Diamond was twenty-one and had no children. She also worked at the post office as a government employee.

She entered Cheyenne's room with six bouquets of flowers, three teddy bears and a card. She was wearing a gray fitted Nike tech and some cool grey 11 Jordan's.

"Damn bitch did somebody die? Your brother inspired you with that outfit?" Chey replied, even though she couldn't help but laugh.

"Shut up. Where is my niece at, why is she not in the room with you?"

"What time is it?" she asked, completely ignoring Diamond's question but not intentionally.

"2:48." Diamond answered

Cheyenne clarified the reason Angela was not allowed into the room along with her. She also described how she ended up in the hospital in the initial instance. How did she get to study for the test, which is due in the next month, and then have to face the whole thing? Chey and Diamond had a close relationship and shared the kind of friendship that any woman would like to have with their boyfriend's sister. They smoked at parties, ate together, and even talked shit about Tyrell together. The moment that Diamond began to date her boyfriend James just six months ago was the time when she and Chey started to drift away from one another.

As Diamond began to put together the tables containing all of Chey's toys and flowers, she was in deep reflection. She was sad because her brother was not there to support her.

"I simply want you to know that my brother is extremely fond of you and my niece extremely."

Chey was aware that Tyrell was having a problem. They've never spent a full day without speaking to one another, particularly now that she was expecting. He barely stayed for an hour without checking on her. He would always ask her whether she needed anything.

"Whatever Diamond, help me get up so that we can take a trip to the nursery. My baby is yet to meet one of her parents. "

"What do you mean?" I thought you could go to the nursery any time, "she asked. She was perplexed.

I could, but I'm in pain. I suffered an urgent C-section. " "What the hell, you didn't get to see Angela in the morning?"

"NO."

Diamond immediately stopped what she was doing with the flowers and attempted to assist her. She followed exactly what Toya did as well as Steph did, but it didn't help. At this point, the pain medication was supposed to kick in, and Chey attempted to sit up quickly. The meds were not doing anything to her. She felt like she needed all the pain medications. It was very difficult for her to leave the bed, and she did not know what to do.

"Call the nurses and request for help," she asked Diamond.

The time flew by, and two nurses arrived in the room. "You have such beautiful flowers," one of them said.

"Thank you, can you please help me get up?" Chey asked both. She didn't mean to be rude, but she felt as if everything was going wrong for her. Throughout her whole pregnancy she tried to make sure things were perfect. She never would have thought this would be her experience having her first child.

Diamond and the nurses tried to help Chey move from her bed. This was difficult for Cheyenne, who weighed 135 pounds. After about ten minutes of struggling, she finally got up. She was so happy and didn't seem to care much about what was happening outside the hospital. She was excited to be able to see her daughter, and that's all that she wanted.

"Thank you so much, take a bouquet of flowers," she insisted to the nurse

Diamond looked at her as if she were crazy, but she didn't say anything.

She replied, "Thank you, but no, take them back. They are beautiful."

Diamond took the wheelchair from her and began to walk toward the nursery. It was overwhelming to feel the joy and excitement that Chey felt inside. Each baby had a name tag that identified the sex and last name of the infant. Before reading the name tag, she recognized

Angela. She was Tyrell's twin. The ventilator was connected to her, and she looked both uncomfortable and comfortable. She was lying so peacefully, and there were so many wires coming from the machine. Toya didn't lie about her baby size. Her tiny arms and hands were adorable. Diamond stared at her, and you could see that she was in love with her niece immediately. Her smile and adorable expression made her think she was beautiful.

"Will you like to hold her?" Nurse Rodriguez asked

Chey noticed her name written on her lab coat when she walked up to them. Her lab coat was unique and must have been the head nurse.

They both replied "Yes" simultaneously.

Diamond mentioned, "I see she's hooked-up to all these machines, but it was not clear if I could hold on to her,"

"Yes, she is being monitored, but she has been breathing independently, so it's okay for us to take her out," nurse Rodriguez stated.

Angela was placed in Chey's arms by Nurse Rodriguez. She stared at Chey and began to cry. Because Tyrell wasn't there, she was unsure if her tears were of joy or sadness. She loved her baby so deeply and wanted to be the best mother she could be. All her worry about Tyrell was gradually turning to anger. Why is he not here with my child? She doesn't need anyone but me, she said to herself. Baby

Angela opened her eyes and looked at her mother before returning to sleep. Aunt Lee used the expression that meant that she was talking to the angels.

Diamond held her for a few minutes before they left the room. Chey held Angela for a second time, and then she kissed her goodnight. It was obvious that she wasn't ready for her to go, and it is quite possible she didn't want to wrestle to get back into bed.

They noticed more flowers at the desk when they got to the room.

They were from the men on the block. The men would always show love, even if they never leave the hood.

CONFESSION

C hey my brother was the one who killed Rich," Diamond said whispering and trembling. He said something about Rich and Tyesha arguing in the hallway, and he told Rich that he needed to go outside to cool down. Rich advised him to mind his business, and the heated exchanges continued.

She starred at Diamond, speechless. It was obvious that she wanted to weep. She felt both hurt and disgusted because he didn't mind his own business. She thought.

She reached for the tissue and asked, "Why didn't he call?

And where is he now? "

"My mom is driving him upstate to her ex-boyfriend." He was then supposed to get him to Miami.

"MIAMI."

"Chey, be quiet." He is going to call you from a burner phone when they get situated. "

"So, the plan was for you to tell me, that's what you were saying?" she asked sarcastically

"No, I was not supposed to tell anyone; he will call you once they are situated and tell you everything. He figured the less you know the better."

She couldn't keep her tears from falling. There was too much going on at once. She recently had a baby and is supposed to be extremely happy right now. Her boyfriend who is also her daughter's father killed a man for another female and now he's on the run heading to Miami. At the age of twenty, with a part time job while studying for her GED were hitting her at once. All she had was her sister who herself was experiencing baby daddy drama.

"I'm tired Diamond I need to go sleep," she said sadly

"Please act like you know nothing, please," she asked while giving Chey a hug and then slowly exiting her room continually looking back like a lost puppy. Chey then texted Toya and Stephanie and told them to come tomorrow and that the nurse was very helpful. She wasn't ready to tell them the exact details about Tyrell just yet.

Today Cheyenne will be able to go home. You can see that she is extremely depressed. She seemed as if she hadn't slept in a while and just mentioned she still hadn't heard from Tyrell or his mom. Her daughter was in this world for only 48 hours and she was already having regrets.

"You're too young to have children."

"Get married first or find your own place." Does he have good credit? Can he get a job? "

All the questions that her aunt Lee's friends had asked her when they found out she was pregnant were running through her mind. But she was in love with Tyrell and he was somewhat taking care of her so she figured she had it all planned out. Her plan was to immediately go to college after her GED. Things weren't going the way she planned. She had one hundred and thirty-five dollars in her wallet. Luckily baby Angela had enough clothes and pampers until she was about six months. Tyrell had some cash at the house, but she never touched his money. He also had some drugs there. She was receiving her maternity check from her part-time job Cookies department store which wasn't much at all. She didn't know what she was going to do, especially when the plan was for Tyrell to watch Angela when she went back to work. His mother was a party promoter and they didn't have the best relationship. Her babysitting Angela wasn't even an option.

"You are going home today," Toya said loudly and excitedly as she entered the room. She had Angela's car seat along with the baby bag, which looked more like a suitcase.

"She going to Miami with her father?" Chey asked sarcastically. One thing for sure they all had smartass mouths.

"TYRELL IN MIAMI!"

"SHH be quiet. He's on the run"

Toya was stunned. She could not open her mouth for more than five seconds before she was able to speak. She then reached Chey and gave her a hug. Toya was also a single mother but she and Dontae were now learning how to co-parent. Also, Dontae family had a good relationship with Toya.

"I packed her three outfits because I didn't know which one you will like," Toya mentioned changing the subject.

Chey was both physically and emotionally in pain. Part of Chey wanted to stay in the hospital, as she knew that going home would only make things worse. She was embarrassed to leave the hospital alone without Tyrell. She deleted all her social media accounts because she didn't want anyone to reach out to her. What was she supposed to say?

Angela was brought by the nurse along with the discharge papers. Cheyenne began to dress Angela and then stared at her. It was as if she thought her daughter was perfect. She was already feeling honored to be her mother. She worried about her future and how she would give the world to her. It is amazing how your entire mindset changes once you have children. Although she wasn't certain if it was her new role as a mom or her current situation, she knew that she needed to find out.

Toya stated, "Dontae & Darren outside. Stephanie said that she will meet us at our house when she gets off of work."

Just like Chey always preached about Dontae, he had his ways, but he is there when they need him. He was the man of their little family. Any repairs, tv mounts, paint jobs he was the one that will fix it. He's very controlling at times and that's another reason he and Toya didn't work out. Sucker shit!!Darren was so excited to meet his baby cousin Angela as he saw them walking towards the car.

He jumped up and down, asking, "She's coming home with us aunty?"

"Yes, baby, she's coming home with us." "Where's uncle Tyrell? She looks like him."

What does she tell a four-year-old? That question caught her by surprise and she wasn't ready to answer. She can avoid the social media questions but what about the people that actually see her. I guess some things you can't escape. She didn't want to lie to him because that will only cause more confusion...you know kids don't forget shit.

"I don't know, baby. I have not heard from him." "HE LEFT YOU." This fucking boy don't have no filter she thought to herself.

"Help your mother put the bags in the car."

Cheyenne couldn't stop crying as they drove home. It was one of those cries that kept your nose running. Because her nephew was in the vehicle, she didn't want to make it obvious. Although she wasn't sure Dontae knew, the thought of explaining it all was making her weep even more. *How did Toya ask him to come get them?* She thought to herself. Everyone knew Tyrell owned two cars.

They pulled up to their building and saw a black Impala car double-parked. This means that the detective team was inside one of the apartments in the building.

Chey shouted, "Oh lord, what's happening in our building now?"

Toya and Dontae ignored her, not really caring what was going on. They lived on the fourth floor with no elevator. Thank God Dontae was with them because Angela and her car seat alone were so heavy. Of course, Darren ran up the stairs with absolutely nothing in his hands. Not even a bag.

"AUNTY THE POLICE ARE HERE FOR YOU."

Darren yelled from the fourth floor.

Toya and Dontae gave each other a look. She walked upstairs slowly, in pain still from the C-section and staples that were still inside of her. Unfortunately, for proper healing they don't get removed until after one week.

"Hi detective, how are you?" Chey asked with shortness of breath.

"Hi, my name is Detective Tavarez, and this is Officer Drummond. We would like to ask you some questions about a shooting on Main Street."

"Why when I live on Carol Street?"

"Can we come in and look around. Ask a few questions?"

She was aware of her rights and knew that she didn't have to let them in. Especially without a warrant. Even though she was feeling overwhelmed and didn't know what to say, she didn't have anything to hide.

"Sure, come in!"

Detective Tavarez asked Chey a few questions about her relationships with Rich, Tyesha, and Tyrell. Chey said that she didn't know much about Rich and Tyesha and that Tyrell was the father of her child. Officer Drummond was moving about, but it was clear that he was looking for something.

"Where is he at now?" Detective asked

"I'm not sure, we had an argument about 4 days ago and I haven't heard from since."

"So, you didn't call him to tell him you had his baby?" "No, he said he didn't want to have anything to do with us."

"That will be it for now," she said as she started walking towards the door. Officer Drummond was giving Chey a strange look as he excited the apartment.

Her first two nights at home were sleepless. Anyone who said that newborns sleep all day was lying. Angela would get up for a bottle every two hours, but it felt like she was getting up every ten minutes. She would get up in the middle of the night and stay up for quite a while. She was most tired at times. It was almost as if Chey had her day and night mixed up. She would stay up all night and sleep all day. Due to depression and lack of sleep, her appetite changed. It was all different. And to think that this was just the beginning was more depressing.

⊷═══════◁•▷◇═══════⊷

"Wake up, Sandra, in the living room." Toya shakes Chey to wake her.

Cheyenne popped up instantly and went straight to the living room area without even having to brush her teeth or wash her face.

Sandra asked, "Where is my grand baby?" Chey replied, "Excuse me!"

"Listen Tyrell will call you on this phone in about ten minutes, he will explain everything to you." she was explaining as she handed Chey a cell phone.

"I already know what happened, the cops were here looking for him regarding a murder."

"What did you tell them? I hope you didn't say anything that could hurt my son." Chey stared at her with a moment of silence and then told her to get out.

"Get out now!"

Not surprisingly at all she stood up, looked Chey up and down and exited the apartment. She only stopped by because Tyrell asked to.

Cheyenne didn't have the strength to argue with her that morning. They never had the best relationship because Sandra felt Tyrell loved Chey more than her and Diamond. She was aware of his fast lifestyle and promoted his illegal activity from a young age. Chey didn't understand why she didn't encourage him to finish school or at least obtain a job.

Tyrell called Chey a little over ten minutes after his mother left.

"Chey, I fucked up, I can't say too much over the phone, but I won't be able to see you and Angela for a while," Tyrell said sobbing

"What do you mean, why can't we meet you?"

Tyrell explained to her why it wasn't a good idea for her and baby Angela to come down to Miami so soon. He wanted them to live comfortably. He explained that he had a plan and she just needed to be patient for about a year or two. She and Tyrell talked on the phone for hours that day and they did video chat so he could see Angela. Seeing Angela made him tear up, realizing his mistake affected all of them. He tried to stay strong for Chey, but he could barely stay strong for himself. He told her he had six thousand dollars in cash at her house that he gave to her.

Even though Tyrell was not physically with them, that talk had calmed Chey's nerves down. She felt relieved to hear his voice and know that he was okay.

FIND YOURSELF

C hey someone is at the door for you, Toya screamed. Cheyenne was in the room with Angela watching law and order. She knew Stephanie was at work so it couldn't have been her. She put on her house robe to hide the stains on her shirt from her leaking nipples.

"Officer Drummond, what are you doing here?" she asked shockingly. He didn't have on any uniform, so he looked a little different. *He looks like somebody from around the way*, not a cop she thought.

"Can I come in and talk to you?" officer Drummond suggested. As she let him in she wasn't sure why he was there. *Does he know I was on the phone with Tyrell for hours and I lied to him and the detective?* She was asking herself

"When detective Tavarez and I came here, I found something that could have gotten you into some serious trouble."

She was confused and asked, "What was it?" Then he sat up and walked to Chey's bedroom.

She said, "My daughter is asleep in there," as she walked faster behind him.

He continued to walk towards her bedroom, and he opened her closet door. Three sneaker boxes contained drugs. Tyrell's drugs were in Cheyenne's closet; she completely forgot.

"Why are you looking through my closet in the first place? You were supposed to be looking for the bathroom." "You have more than enough drugs in here to get charged and that's what you care about? I know these aren't your drugs, they belong to Tyrell. I advise you to flush everything down the toilet because they will be back to look for him and this time it won't be just the two of us. Make sure the murder weapon is not in here as well," Officer Drummond stated

"Murder Weapon!"

"Ms. Brown, your boyfriend, will be arrested and charged with murder." Drummond suggested that if he didn't have anything to hide, he could come down to the station to answer some questions.

"Get out my house now," she demanded as she pointed towards the door.

"Listen you are a new mom of a beautiful daughter, don't let this man ruin your life and then who will raise your daughter? I came here on my own because I genuinely want to help you."

"You don't even know me, or are you one of those cops that genuinely wants to help your community?" She said sarcastically.

Officer Drummond just looked at her and then handed her his business card and walked himself out. She looked at the card and put it in the same kitchen drawer with the food menus. Cheyenne immediately called Tyrell hoping he would pick up.

"Hey baby, are you okay?" he answered

"Yes, I am okay, what are you going to do with these drugs in the closet?"

"I'm going to have my mom come get it."

She explained to Tyrell that his mother needs to come pick it up as soon as possible but she didn't tell him about the cop. She didn't want him to worry more than he already was.

Tyrell called Cheyenne back explaining to her that his mother wasn't coming to pick up the drugs. She didn't ask why because she assumed she already knew.

"So, what do you want me to do?" she asked him. "Give me a week and I will let you know, but I must call you back. Kiss Angela for me and I love you." Click. He didn't wait for Cheyenne to reply. She then went into the room with Toya and Darren and suggested they have a family night. Popcorn and wine, she wanted something to feel like her old self before all the drama.

"I'll make sure to tell Stephanie to stop by after work," Toya stated while texting her.

Stephanie lived with her mother Debra and older brother Joe. Her mom was ill, and her brother was never home. When Joe did come home, he would steal from them and then disappear again. Debra was sick since Stephanie was 16 years old and couldn't work by the time she was 17. At 18 Stephanie finished high school and started working for the city as a school safety agent and has been paying the bills since. She and Chey were the same age and had been friends since they were in elementary school fourth grade.

<hr />

Cheyenne was in a better space for herself and Angela. She was getting the hang of Angela's schedule.

She was eager to take her GED exam the following day. Angela was in the swing, quiet as a mouse while she was studying. Chey was ready to start college and find a better job to start her new life. Setting an example for Angela was her only priority.

Chey and Tyrell talked on the phone every day and Diamond would come to see Angela approximately three times a week.

Stephanie would sleep over some nights to help as well, and Toya would plan family night once a week. She started to feel like herself again but there were still some nights she cried herself to sleep. Her friends and family just couldn't fill the void in her heart from Tyrell.

RESPONSIBILITY

They noticed a stressful expression on Toya's face as she was walking to the kitchen to prepare Angela bottles. "What's wrong girl I see something wrong with you?" Chey asked Toya in a concerned way.

"Dontae lost his job and now he can't pay for Darren's childcare."

Having a kid at a young age you don't think about any of this. You don't think about how much it costs financially to raise a child or how much time you must set aside for your child. Cheyenne thought about the drugs she had in her closet and how Sandra wasn't coming for it.

"I have three pounds of marijuana in the closet, do he want to flip it?" Chey suggested.

"Hell No, he is not into that. He wouldn't even know where to start." Toya answered

"Okay it was just a suggestion, damn," she answered. Cheyenne has been home a month now and spent a little more than two thousand dollars. She paid her half of rent for two months and also went shopping for clothes. All her clothes were too big from the pregnancy. She knew she had to figure something out soon. She wasn't ready to go back to work anytime soon but the way things were looking she might have to put Angela in daycare sooner than she thought.

Today was the day Cheyenne took her GED exam and she was exhausted. Stephanie was supposed to watch Angela today but her job called her in to work. Chey called Diamond last minute and she told her to bring Angela to her boyfriend's house. When she arrived, she saw two guys leaving the apartment walking towards a Range Rover. She was already uncomfortable leaving Angela there but what other choice did she have. Toya was working doubles almost every day. Diamond's boyfriend answered the door, and he was old enough to be her father. She couldn't believe that it was Diamond's boyfriend. Diamond came running to the door excited to watch her niece grabbing the car seat and baby bag out Chey hand.

"Good luck with your test girl, you got this!" she shouted.

Chey was contemplating how she could improve herself as she took a taxi to the testing location. She imagined that she would get her GED and then go to college to become an educator. She had always wanted to achieve this dream.

While I'm in college I will get a better paying job to help me get a car and buy a house, she thought

When she arrived at the site, the line to enter was just around the corner. Chey almost lost her eyes when she saw Sandra already in line. Sandra stared at her but didn't speak a word. You wouldn't have thought Cheyenne was the mother of Sandra's granddaughter. She continued walking to the back of the line, not even bothering to speak a word. After waiting in line for twenty-five minutes, she was finally allowed to enter the building. She began the exam about forty minutes later. Before answering the first question, she prayed to God.

As everyone left, the instructor said to them: "Check your email in six weeks for your results."

She was thrilled to finish her exam and pick up Angela. It was one of those feelings when you feel like you can't live with them but also can't live without them. She then called Tyrell to tell him how confident she felt about passing her GED, but he didn't answer.

Toya and Dontae were sitting on the couch as Chey, and Angela entered the apartment.

"We are about to have a family meeting?" Chey asked when she saw Dontae. She hasn't seen Dontae sit in the living room for years. He usually only comes for Darren.

"Yea we actually are, Dontae wants to talk to you." Toya said as she reached for Angela from Chey's arms.

Dontae was interested in selling the marijuana Chey had in the closet. This was a new concept for him, so Chey taught him what Tyrell taught her. Dontae was very interested in numbers and profits. He would make more every week than he made at his previous job. He agreed to sell, and Chey's plan was to have everything set up that night.

When Chey and Dontae finished talking she went into Toya's room to get Angela but they both were already sleeping that quick. Toya worked for the Office of Mental Health so her schedule was everywhere.

FALLING INTO PLACE

Stephanie arrived early in the morning to bring breakfast and a toy for Darren. Because she couldn't relax at home, this house was a source of peace of mind. Chey didn't expect to see Steph when she awoke, but she was happy to find that she had bought food.

"I'm starving, what did you bring?" Chey asked.

She opened the bag to discover bacon, sausages, eggs, French toast, and pancakes. It's enough to feed at most ten people.

"Damn girl you hit the lotto." Toya said walking out the bathroom as she heard them taking everything out of the bag.

"Something like that." she said as she dropped a Nissan Altima key on the table.

"Bitch! I'm so proud of you!" Chey said

Toya gave her a hug and didn't say anything. The joy Toya had for Stephanie, she felt it with her hug. Stephanie explained to them why she wasn't coming over as much and was always at work. She told her supervisor that if any overtime became available that she would take it. She worked overtime every day for two months straight, sometimes coming in on her off days. When you really want to achieve something, you must put in a lot of effort. Chey was delighted to see the growth in her best friend and that only motivated her more to obtain her driver's license and purchase a vehicle of her own.

It was 9:53am and Toya realized she needed to get ready for work. Darren was staying home with Chey and Angela because he had a doctor's appointment. Chey agreed to take him because she knew Toya needed the money. Steph offered to drive them which was a big help. On the way heading to the doctor Dontae called stating that he needs more weed because he sold it all.

Damn he finished that quick, she thought to herself.

Angela sobbed the entire time they were at the doctor's office. Chey was kicking herself for taking Darren when Toya went to work. She began to feel as if she was going to have a nervous breakdown. She had just fed and changed Angela's diaper, so she had no idea why she was crying. She began to think about Tyrell and how he had put himself in a position where he couldn't help her. Angela's only respite had been when she went to take her GED exam or when Toya had her in the room with her at times. Tyrell was calling her at the time.

Tyrell hadn't been heard from in two days, so she was relieved to hear he was fine. She revealed to him that Dontae was assisting her in selling the marijuana because his mother had not arrived. He wasn't upset and thought it was a fantastic idea. He advised her she should acquire some more after Dontae sells everything in the closet so she wouldn't have to rush back to work. She reasoned that it was a good idea because she wanted to concentrate on her studies.

Dontae handed Chey twenty-four hundred dollars, with eight hundred being his profit. Chey began to wonder how she could get used to this. Dontae aimed to become a music producer, so he felt he could spend more time in the studio working on his music as well. She gave Dontae all the marijuana she had left and asked him if it would be a good idea to sell it or if he was still looking for a job. He didn't even put in applications that week because he was so busy in the studio.

"My goal is to get Toya and Darren into a more prominent place so he can have his own room. He is growing up fast. Working with you I can probably get the money faster," he explained to Chey.

She was pleased that he agreed but she never considered Toya leaving that apartment. Then she would have to pay rent and everything by herself.

Chey called Steph to pick her up when she got off work to treat her to dinner. After having Angela, she wanted to dress up and wear heels for the first time. She decided that her, Darren and Angela were going to wear all black like a family. Toya was on the double, so Chey was babysitting throughout the day. Although she could have called Dontae, it was not big of a deal as Angela was still with her. She took a bath using her Dr. Bronner's peppermint soap. The tingling she felt on her body was relaxing and the smell was awesome. She would never use it for her vagina area, she then switched to the dove sensitive soap for that area. She then reached for her rose clit vibrator.

"I knew I had to wait six weeks after having Angela, not almost 6 months" she said out loud sarcastically.

As she relaxed, she laid back and closed her eyes.

She lit her blunt and began playing with herself. The sensation from the vibrator was remarkable. She started reminiscing how Tyrell would eat her out and then slide his penis inside of her and then lick up all her juices. The memories and the speed of her toy made her cum quicker.

"Aunty, Angela is up, she is crying." Darren yelled

Cheyenne put her blunt out and stood up quickly to rinse off the water. She sprayed the bathroom really quickly and ran out to Angela.

After feeding and changing Angela, Chey was ready to get dressed. She wore a black Gucci shirt dress with her Gucci stockings and Gucci platform boots. Angela was wearing her Gucci dress and shoes that Diamond bought her, and Darren had on a black Chrome heart sweat suit with his Jordan sneakers. They were all looking cute, but they now had to wait for Steph's arrival to pick them up. While they waited outside for Steph, Chey noticed a black police car parked two houses down. However, she pretends like she didn't see them.

Steph pulled up blasting music looking beautiful as always with her thirty-inch wig. She assisted Chey with Angela and Chey helped Darren put on his car seat. As they arrived at red lobsters, Tyesha was the first person Chey noticed. She was sitting at the bar with another guy. This was the first time Chey saw her since Tyrell killed her boyfriend.

"Table for 3 and a highchair." the waitress asked us.

"Table for four is fine, no highchair required." Chey replied. Chey knew Angela was too small for the highchair and she needed that extra space on the side for Angela's car seat. She was hoping she would have to walk past Tyesha so that she noticed her.

"Right this way." the waitress stated as she started walking towards the bar.

As Chey got closer to Tyesha she realized she had seen the guy before. He was with Tyrell a couple of times. *So, my boyfriend is on the run for helping her dumb ass and now she in red lobster with another man already* she thought.

As the waiter sat them down Darren requested for some biscuits. "Aunty, can I order crab legs?" he asked Chey. "Okay." she said with a slightly sarcastic attitude. Although she was not mad at Darren, her night was ruined by Tyesha. She was overwhelmed by emotions and began to hate Tyrell.

"What's wrong with you?" Steph asked her.

"Nothing, just tired a little bit." Chey replied. "Bitch you are not tired, is everything ok with Tyrell? Did you and him have an argument?"

"F Tyrell." Chey said aggressively.

"Yea I know what that means." Steph said as she grabbed her menu. Chey tried to enjoy the rest of the night, but her mind wouldn't allow her to. She received a text message from Dontae stating that he needed to see her.

She just gave Dontae the last weed she had right before they went to dinner. *There was no way he could have finished all of that already, she* thought to herself. I mean that would be the only reason he wants to see her though. Chey told him they could talk the following day when he picked Darren for school. Surprisingly after Chey had a sip of wine she didn't think about Tyesha or Tyrell for the rest of dinner.

Chey and Toya sat down, talking in the kitchen the next day before Dontae arrived. Toya said that she was looking for a larger apartment. Darren was growing up and needed more space. Chey didn't know what she could afford, as she didn't have a steady income. She wanted to quit Cookies and attend school full-time. It would take her forever to get her degree going to school part-time she figured. Dontae knocked at the door right after Darren had finished his breakfast. Dontae immediately threw the cash on the counter.

She shouted, "Damn, you finished already!" in shock. He replied, "Yeah, the guys in the studio smoke heavily."

"Damn, they do not play. I do not have any more." as she picked up the phone to call Tyrell.

Toya was given five hundred dollars by Dontae. He had already paid the fees for daycare. Toya was surprised that it wasn't her birthday, but she didn't complain. Dontae had given her money to help her save for a car, so she didn't spend it. She put it aside for savings.

Tyrell felt relieved when Chey explained the situation. It was good to know Chey and Angela were well taken care of. Angela didn't need any financial assistance at all right now. He wanted her back to school because he knew that she was smart and wanted her to be an example to their daughter. Tyrell gave Chey some guy's number named Malik and told her to meet him later. He was supposed to give her more marijuana.

She later met Malik while Dontae babysat Angela. She almost choked as she approached the store. He was the same guy who was with Tyesha in red lobsters. She gave fifty dollars to the taxi driver and promised him that she would return. He waited patiently, as it was only a ten-dollar ride. They went into the corner store, and she introduced herself. Chey followed Malik down the aisle, walking all the way to the back. The downstairs was completely different, with a couch and flat-screen TV. But you could see that no one lived there. She thought so, at least. There were five shelves long, and there was nothing but drugs and other supplies. She gave him the money, and he gave Chey a bag with drugs. As she walked towards the door, she was relieved to see that the taxi didn't leave the store.

Angela was asleep when Chey returned home. Since he was with Toya, Chey and Dontae had always been friends. She just didn't respect some of the things he put her sister through as any family member wouldn't. She gave Dontae weed. He explained to her that he would have enough money by the end of the month to buy Toya an automobile. He decided to help her get a car before he got a larger apartment. She knew Dontae was still in love with Toya. However, he cheated on Toya with his ex-girlfriend. Toya couldn't forgive him. She stated that she might have looked past the girl if it were a new girl but that this particular girl had hurt her. Chey thought that she should also take driving lessons so she could get her driver's license. Tyrell drove her everywhere, and if that wasn't possible, he would take her to a taxi. Since Tyrell and Chey became exclusive, she never used public transport.

"Let me get out of here and make this money." Dontae said as he was leaving.

Chey woke up to a new notification on her phone.

She shouted, "I passed," and ran around the house screaming. Angela woke up crying. Toya was at work while Darren was in school. She called Stephanie. "Girl! I passed my GED, so I can officially go to college."

Stephanie started screaming on the other end. "Congratulations girl I knew you were going to pass."

She spoke to Stephanie about Dontae's weekly income. That morning Chey was feeling good, like she did not have a worry in the world.

"Let me get back to work and I'll call you on my lunch break" Steph said as they hung up.

She then called Tyrell to tell him the news. He was more excited than her and she just wished she could have seen him. She wanted to be in his arms so bad. Chey almost had twenty-five thousand saved and her rent was paid for the next six months. Her road test was scheduled in two weeks.

Tyrell was doing well for himself out in Miami. He told Chey when things calmed down and he got his own place that her and Angela could come down. But he didn't know she was already thinking about surprising him for his birthday in July before she starts school in August.

Toya called Cheyenne screaming of excitement.

Dontae had purchased her a car and paid down the mortgage on a house for her. She was shocked but happy to hear her sister's joy. Toya had to leave work early in order to pack her belongings and Darren's.

Chey was happy and sad all at once. Although she was thrilled that Darren would have his own room, the thought of Angela and her alone made her sad. Toya helped Chey and Angela with their family nights, which helped with her depression.

Sometimes when Toya was at work, she would feel lonely and depressed until she came home. Toya would even take Angela sometimes in the middle of the night so Chey could sleep longer. Her primary support was leaving, and, in that moment, she felt abandoned again. Dontae called Chey to share the good news with her. He also informed her that he would pay Toya's rent for six more months, even though she was leaving with Darren. Even though she could afford the bills, he didn't want Chey to pay all the bills by herself.

She said to him, "Thanks, Dontae. I appreciate that." She was even more determined to return to school, knowing her rent had been paid for one year.

Toya and Darren arrived home thirty minutes later. Toya ran to Chey, shouting, "Thanks, thank you, if this wasn't for you, it wouldn't be happening." Toya was jumping around.

Chey jokes, "Girl, if it weren't for Tyrell,"

"Are you going to help me pack? Dontae will be here at 6 to take us.

"Yea I guess, do I really have a choice?" Chey replied. They had plenty of time to pack everything since it was only two o'clock in the afternoon. Toya just wanted to pack everything in her bedroom.

Toya stated, "When you move out and if you don't take the living room or kitchen set, I'll come back for it."

Chey responded, "OK, it's all yours."

Toya couldn't throw out Aunt Lee's living room and kitchen set. She wanted everything she could get that was a part of her.

While Chey was cleaning her drawers, she looked around and saw how she could arrange her bed in Toya's room. Because it was more significant, she knew she was going to make that her room. Angela could then have her own space. Chey was excited with the thought of decorating Angela's bedroom. It might not be as difficult as she imagined.

They were almost done by the time it reached four thirty.

Toya began cooking tacos while Chey made margaritas.

Chey started hearing the phone ring in her ear through her air pod. As if she were able to see who was calling, she ran to the back and began running. She recognized it to be either Tyrell, or Stephanie.

It was Tyrell and she smiled showing all her teeth as she answered the phone.

"I miss you," he said as she answered.

She was lying in bed and began talking to Tyrell. She was telling Tyrell everything about Toya's new house and what was happening. Everything was perfect, except for Tyrell not being there physically to support Angela and her. Toya walked into Chey's bedroom after ten minutes.

"Did you forget you have a daughter and margaritas out here," she said annoyingly. Toya hated when Chey and Tyrell talked on the phone, because she would sometimes act like the world stopped. She is so focused on the phone that she forgets anything else.

Chey hung up on Tyrell as she said, "I love you, baby." I'll call you later. "

She enjoyed her tacos and then fell asleep with Angela.

Chey woke up to find that the clock was showing 11:52 pm.

She exclaimed, "Damn, I slept all night." She looked up to see that Angela had left her crib and that Toya was still there. She didn't know that she would see people in her living room as she went to the bathroom. Then she noticed Toya crying in Dontae's mother's arm while Dontae's brother Darius was holding Angela.

Toya cried, "They killed him."

Chey was shocked and just stood there as if she was peeing on herself. Although her mouth was open, she didn't speak as though she wanted to, but she couldn't.

She finally asked, "Where, Why, how?" and immediately began to cry.

Darius said, "It had been someone he trusts because he was shot, then thrown out the car, and he bled out."

Shey snatched Angela from him and said, "OMG!" Darius was crying when she said, "Thank you for holding Angela down."

As she reached out to hug Toya, she said, "I'm so sorry for your loss Toya." Toya could not stop crying, and Chey hadn't seen her this way since Aunt Lee's passing.

Darren was asleep in the back. She was unsure if he knew or not. Both Darius and Toya were in great pain.

She started crying again as she entered the bedroom to change Angela's diaper. She felt guilty as her tears began to fall like a rainfall. Dontae was a hardworking man who loved and cared deeply for his son. He also had a job. Chey was aware that Dontae's selling of drugs was a factor in his death.

Chey decided to call Tyrell to see if maybe he heard anything. He explained to her that he had heard Dontae was killed but didn't hear who did it.

"Why didn't you call to check on me if you heard?" she asked him.

He explained to her that he was busy completing paperwork for his apartment and he planned to call her later. She felt it was bullshit, but she was too hurt to argue.

"I'll call you tomorrow," she told him. That was one night that felt like it would never end.

Chey made Toya breakfast the next morning. Toya was still sitting at the same exact spot from the night before. Dontae's mom took Darren with her. Toya was always grateful for the love and support they gave to Darren.

She told Toya to eat something as she set the plate on the table.

Toya looked at her and shook her head. She then said, "I'm not hungry."

Chey didn't insist that she didn't want to eat the food. She knew that her sister was hurt, and there was nothing she could do.

"Let's see the house he purchased for you and Darren." Although she wasn't sure if it was too early to bring it up, she tried getting Toya off the couch. Toya shook her head again, but this time she didn't say much. Both of them sat down on the couch until shortly after someone knocked. Chey opened the door to find Stephanie. Cheyenne and Stephanie stared blankly at each other as if they could guess each other's thoughts.

Stephanie whispered in Chey's ear, "A vacation is calling us."

Stephanie was there to babysit Angela and also support Toya. Chey felt uncomfortable leaving Toya for an hour to do her driving lesson but she couldn't reschedule it. She had to pass her road test in two weeks.

Toya was not there when Chey returned home.

Stephanie explained to Toya that Darius had come to pick Stephanie up to show her the house. She was thrilled to hear that she was now out of the house. Toya and Chey had planned their trip to Miami. They all needed it. Chey also still had drugs in her closet that Dontae didn't get a chance to finish.

"What should I do with this?" Chey asked Steph as she showed her the four Ziploc bags of marijuana.

"Give it to me. Steph laughed and said that I'm going to smoke it.

Stephanie convinced Chey to sell it back to Malik, she had bought it from him. She decided it was worth trying and called a taxi. Because she knew Stephanie was busy, and she didn't intend to ask Toya to babysit Angela anytime soon, this was the best time for her to handle everything.

She was practicing how to ask him if he would like to buy his weed back throughout the entire taxi ride. She figured she would ask him to only give her half, that sounds more reasonable. She was giving him Dontae's half and she took some out for Stephanie.

Cheyenne did her normal thing and handed the driver a fifty-dollar bill and asked him if he would wait for her. She felt nervous as she got out of the taxi and entered the store. She didn't know what his reaction was going to be. Although she thought of calling Tyrell several times to ask him questions, she was still somewhat upset by him.

"Miss please put your hands where I can see them and turn around slowly," an Officer said out loud as Chey was entering the store.

Her heart could have hit the floor and rolled over when she heard a cop behind her. She knew she had marijuana on her as well and all she could think about was Angela. She turned around slowly and saw Officer Drummond.

"What's inside the bag?" Officer Drummond asked her.

"My work clothes, I want to get some food before I go," she replied nervously.

"I think that you should go to another store for food," he told

her.

She said, "OK," as she began to walk faster toward the taxi.

She was shaking and trembling as she headed home. If she went to jail, Chey couldn't picture Angela not being held or seeing her. All of the money she'd saved would have to be paid to a lawyer.

She thought to herself that everything was going well the week before. Dontae is then killed and she is almost arrested all within the same week.

Chey throws the duffle bag at Stephanie as she enters the house and grabs Angela. She sits down and just adores how precious her daughter was.

"I don't want her to have this kind of life. Let her see the world, and I will do my best for her. We own all the expensive shit, and we have never left the country. Tyrell bought me my first mink coat, but I am still living in an apartment my aunt left for us. I don't have anything, not even a car. Now that Dontae is dead, I may have to return to the Cookies Department store. What else am I going to do without proper education?" Chey vented to Stephanie as she was tearing up.

She couldn't stop thinking about what she would have done if she had gone to jail. Her heart felt sadder for Toya losing Dontae.

"You are doing the best you can with the cards you were dealt with," Stephanie said to Chey as she hugged her.

"Me, you and Toya practically raised ourselves and we are doing a wonderful job. Do not beat yourself up over something you cannot control. You are here raising Angela alone without any physical help from Tyrell and you don't have any family left on top of that. We don't have any role models, we wanted this for ourselves."

Chey thanked Stephanie for her encouraging words as she grabbed Angela and headed back. She called Tyrell to explain to him all that happened, and he was glad to hear that she was okay. Their phone call was interrupted by the doorbell as she then walked to the front to find out who it was. Chey was surprised to see it was Officer Drummond, but this time he had flowers in his hands.

"Hey, what are you doing here?" Chey asked him. "These are for you," he said to her as he was handing her the flowers.

"Can I come in?" he asked.

She was unsure of what was happening and why he had bought her flowers. He just stood there as he came in. It is obvious that he did not intend to stay long. He explained that she needed to stop doing any illegal activity she had been engaging in. There is a case against the men who surround that store. He also explained that Sandra could have been involved in Dontae's death and to be cautious.

"Why are you telling me all of this?" she looked confused and asked.

He said, in a flirty manner, "You and your child deserve a bright future." And hopefully, one day, I will be in it".

Officer Drummond was attracted to Chey and wanted to do everything he could for her. He wanted Angela and Chey to be happy. "Seriously, stay away from over there and I hope to hear from you soon" he said as he opened the door to leave.

She was shocked at what had happened and that a cop was flirting with her. She thought to herself that even if Tyrell and her were to split up, he wouldn't allow her to have a happy relationship with a cop. The thought of her fucking Officer Drummond was getting her wet. It's been over six months since she was last touched, and she felt like she was overdue. Although she thought he was handsome, her love for Tyrell was so strong that no one could ever stop them.

Chey texted Officer Drummond that night to express her gratitude for saving her life. He was thrilled that she reached out.

He said, "To start with, stop calling me Officer Drummond, my name is Amare."

Amare was still working but enjoyed his time with her. They had made arrangements to meet for dinner the next day by the time they ended the call.

MIAMI

They asked Diamond to watch Angela while she and Amare went out to dinner. While she did tell her the restaurant she was going to, she didn't tell her partner.

She wanted to learn more about Dontae's case and whether they were still searching for Tyrell. She knew Amare liked her and was already putting his job at risk for her. He took her to Chart House, a seafood restaurant. They had a great time. As they were getting to know each other she realized that she didn't want to use him. He came from a beautiful family that was very family oriented. That was something her and Toya rarely experienced. His mom left him a three story house before she moved away after she retired from the air force. He was a police officer for nearly four years and had no children. She loved the fact that he had all his shit together at twenty-five. He would remind Chey to never hesitate to ask for help if she ever needed it.

Amare had sent Chey some job applications to work for the government that night. He explained to her his mother was single and worked for the government. She provided him with a positive, fulfilling life. She didn't have to worry about the cops arresting her for illegal activity or the thought of her losing someone she loved daily.

"How is your sister holding up" Amare asked Chey "She is not doing well at all; she hasn't been home since it happened. Why do you think my daughter's grandmother has something to do with it?" You can hear it in his voice that he was hesitating to answer her question.

"We believe that Sandra and Melly hired someone to kill Dontae."

"Melly? She asked, "Who is that?"

"Melly is the guy you were going to see at the store, you mean to tell me you didn't know his name?" he asked her.

She was confused because she didn't know him as Melly, and she wondered what Sandra had to do with anything. She didn't even know Sandra was that close to him. *His government name must be Malik*, she thought to herself.

THREE WEEKS LATER***

Toya, Stephanie, and Chey were thrilled to be going on a girls' trip. Angela was with Diamond at Chey's residence while Darren was visiting his grandma. Tyrell had no idea Chey was coming to Miami, and she couldn't wait to see his expression when she shocked him. Toya really wanted to travel to the beach for some relaxation after Dontae's funeral two weeks ago. "We have to get some nips before we get to the airport," Stephanie yelled. It wasn't a girl's trip if you didn't start pregaming at the airport. It was only ten o'clock in the morning and Aunt Lee used to always say, *Its six o'clock somewhere else right now.*

While Toya and Chey waited in front for the cab, Stephanie dashed to the liquor store around the block. Steph returned just in time for the cab to come. They were officially prepared to leave. The airport was congested, but Jet Blue's line was continually moving. They were all seated in the same row, with Chey in the center and Toya near the window. They all took a shot as the plane began to take off.

They landed in Miami three hours later. They were already taking off their sweaters before they could exit the airport. It was almost 100 degrees in Miami. But it was only sixty-one in New York. Chey enjoyed the moment as they walked out to catch the shuttle bus to their destination. She was shocked to discover Tyrell lived in this beautiful city. The palm trees were the first thing that she fell in love with instantly. She looked at her phone and saw a message from Amare, wishing her a safe flight. He also had sent a picture of an outfit he had bought for Angela.

Chey stated, "He hasn't even met her yet and he spoils her." "Chey had a baby with a drug dealer and was now dating a police officer. Your life is a movie." Stephanie said laughing.

Toya didn't say anything, but you could see that she was thinking about something. Chey thought about the comment she made, and perhaps that led her to think about Dontae's past actions in spoiling Darren. She felt sorry and changed the subject immediately.

Stephanie, who had just finished her third nip, was still stumbling around in the lobby when they arrived at Hilton Miami Airport Blue Lagoon. Chey checked them into the hotel, and the bellmen escorted them to their room. They planned to spend the day at the resort, enjoying the hot tub and pool, before heading to House of Mac for dinner. Chey was eager to surprise Tyrell the next day. They hadn't seen each other in person since she was pregnant.

⬦═══════⬥◀▶▣═══════⬦

Chey woke up the next morning to seven missed calls from Amare. She called him back immediately hoping everything was okay.

He said, "Open your front door," as soon as he answered.

She was confused as he knew she was in Miami, not at home.

She asked, confused, "My front door?" "Yes, you are staying at the Hilton!"

She ran to the front, opening the door to a variety of fruits from edible arrangements, and roses.

"OMG! When did you? How did you do?"

Chey was so overjoyed that she couldn't complete her sentence. She was stunned that he had surprised her all the way in Miami. She loved Amare's gentlemanly demeanor. He would send her gifts and check on her to remind her that he cared about her. He was the best thing for her and she enjoyed his time more than anything. Especially since he was a cop and always had to work overtime. He had planned to take Chey and Angela on a trip, but things were moving so quickly that she wasn't able to confirm it. She was still in love with Tyrell, and she still believed they could be a family without having to look over their shoulders.

"I have to go back to work, babe. I hope you like the flowers and enjoy your girl's trip.

"I love them, you're so nice to me," Chey said as she hung up the phone.

She was really interested in Amare, but she wanted to keep her boundaries. She wanted to make sure that he understood that they were just dating. That is why she did not confirm the trip that he was planning for her and Angela. She felt that was a bit extreme and was not ready to bring him around baby Angela. They would only go on dates while Toya watched Angela or sometimes he'd cook for her and invite her to his house. She never once let him relax in her apartment.

When Chey finished getting dressed, Toya and Stephanie were already in the water. Chey didn't even put on her bathing suit since she wanted to go to Tyrell right away. She was dressed in a floral maxi dress that accentuated her curves. Tyrell liked her in maxi dresses, so she wanted to look her best for him.

She could tell Toya and Stephanie were comfortable and enjoying their margaritas as she approached the pool to pick them up. She simply paused and looked around, grateful for the opportunity to share this moment with them.

Stephanie shouted, "Come on! Are y'all ready?" She laughed and said, "I'm ready to see my man,"

Stephanie jumped out the pool, grabbed her towel, and ran to get out. As she jumped out of the pool, you could see everyone watching. The pink two-piece showed her curves. Toya chose to remain in the pool, telling the girls that she was going to relax at the hotel and that she would see them on the way back. Chey and Stephanie were headed to the rental car when she began to call Tyrell.

"Where are you at?" she asked him.

"I'm at Robby house, what is Angela doing?"

She replied, "She is asleep," not knowing exactly what Angela was doing. "This is Toya, baby. Chey quickly told him that she would call him back. She did not want him to hear her background.

Chey had to send a package to Robby's house one day in the past so that's how she knew his address. They were only eight minutes away when Stephanie entered the address into the GPS.

She was excited to finally see her man after almost a year. Although she wished Angela was there, she knew that they would be able to spend plenty of time together as a family. As soon as they arrived in front of the house Chey's phone started ringing. She thought Tyrell was watching her because he was always a step ahead of anyone when it came to someone popping up on him or trying to surprise him.

As she looked at her phone, she noticed it was Amare. She was too excited to see Tyrell to even pick up the phone.

Stephanie stated, "I'm going to stay in the car while you go knock on the door."

The outside of the house was large and beautiful. Two cars were parked in front, a BMW and a Benz. The garden was vibrant, and the grass was cut short, so it was obvious that someone was taking care of it. She was shocked to discover that this was where Tyrell was staying. Her heart rate increased as she got closer to the front door. Although she didn't understand why she was so nervous, she was.

She rang the bell once and waited less than 30 seconds until someone answered the door.

"Tyesha!!!" Chey yelled, surprised.

Tyrell yelled, "Who is it, baby?" as he ran down the stairs. "Baby!? Chey shouted as she kicked open the front door.

Tyesha tried closing the front door, but Chey's foot was already inside the house.

"Bitch you violated," she shouted to Tyesha as she started punching her in the face. Tyesha immediately fell to the ground, and Chey continued hitting her. Tyrell was shocked at what he saw and couldn't believe his eyes. Chey continued beating up Tyesha. Stephanie ran out of the car heading inside the house but Tyrell grabbed her.

"No, nobody getting jumped," he yelled while holding Stephanie back.

"What the fuck is going on." Stephanie shouted as she tried to let loose from Tyrell's arm.

After Chey had finished beating Tyesha, she spit in Tyrell's face and told Stephanie they should go. Tyesha was lying on the ground, holding her stomach, and crying.

Tyrell looked at Tyesha, wanting to comfort her. But he could not let Chey go unassisted without speaking to her. Cheyenne was devastated about what she had just witnessed. She was overwhelmed by the thoughts that were racing through her mind. Nobody came down to help them, which means Tyesha and Tyrell lived there alone. Tyrell killed Tyesha's boyfriend. Those two cars were theirs. They were just living the life out here while she was struggling in New York with his daughter. She was not willing to believe that any of this was true. Everything happened so quickly.

Stephanie was also confused and shocked by what had happened. She jumped in the driver's seat and began to drive. Tyrell jumped in the silver Mercedes and began following their lead.

"Pull the fuck over," Tyrell shouted as he pulled up on the right side of them.

Stephanie kept on driving as if he were a ghost. Chey didn't even look out the side window. As she gazed out of the front window, she looked as if she was a statue with tears streaming down her face. Tyrell managed to cut his car in front of Stephanie almost causing her to crash.

"Stop the fucking car Steph, I need to talk to Chey." "Fuck you clown, she doesn't want speak to you,

I'm Angela's father now bitch!" Stephanie yelled out the window.

"Stay right here, I'm going to talk to him, I have a plan," Chey said while getting out of the car.

She walked over to Tyrell's vehicle to listen to what he had to say. Tyrell was distraught and reached out for Chey to give him a hug. She backed away almost falling backwards from backing up so fast.

"Don't touch me, what happened?" She asked him. "Chey I'm sorry I can explain," he started.

"There is nothing to really explain, you left our home and family to only start a family out here with this bitch. Tyrell, you never even saw our daughter in person, how could you do this to me?" She stated as her tears were washing down her face.

"No, it wasn't like that, I love you and Angela. He was beating her up and I ran to him with my gun to stop him. As he was walking out the building, he turned around and pointed his gun at me. Although I shot him immediately, I didn't intend to kill him. A week or two later Tyesha called me stating she was scared that Rich's family was going to kill or harm her. I didn't want another body on my hands so we sent her out here. One thing led to another and now we are here. Sorry, Chey, I didn't know what to say, but my heart is with you. She was there to keep me company and help me through the nights and days I wanted to be with you and Angela.

"Hurry up girl, let's enjoy the rest of our vacation!" Stephanie yelled from the car.

"So, this is your life now? This is how you will live forever?

Angela will need to travel to Miami to see her father? How could you do this to us Tyrell? How?" Chey asked him repeatedly.

"I'm only staying here for another month or so and then things will get better. I promise Chey!"

"I'm going to let Stephanie take me back to the hotel, I need to lay down. I have a headache now." Chey replied

"Can we please talk later? Can we go out to eat?

What hotel are you staying at?" Tyrell asked her twenty one questions before she could answer one.

"Tyrell, I'm going to call you tomorrow, give me some time to think everything through. I'm out here for another three days, we can have dinner before I leave."

She returned back to the car trying to hold in her tears. Her heart was pounding so rapidly as if it was ready to jump out. It was embarrassing that Stephanie was there to witness it.

<hr>

Chey was there in the hotel room the entire day ordering room service. Toya was still grieving Dantae's death, so Stephanie made sure Toya had a great time on her vacation. Although Chey loved the pool, her body and mind weren't strong enough for her to enjoy it fully. She was in pain all over again, and she wanted Tyrell to feel the suffering and pain she had been experiencing.

Amare called her, and she explained the situation to him. He was horrified to hear about what Chey was experiencing on her first vacation. Out of anger she was willing to do whatever it took to destroy Tyrell.

"I need you to come down here right away and come lock him up," Chey told Amare

"That is not my jurisdiction, I can't just do that, and besides I want you to think about what you're saying. That is Angela's father at the end of the day. He will eventually get caught and you don't want that on your conscience."

Amare tried to explain, but she was already convinced Amare, I don't care! My daughter and I are trying to figure this out together day by day. He is out here playing house with the next bitch! The same woman who put him in this situation. My sister's boyfriend was basically killed to support Angela and me, while he was just out here living comfortably" she said to him as she began to cry harder.

"If this is something you are serious about, give me his address and I will discuss it over with my boss. We can have Miami PD pick him and transfer him to New York.

Are you sure this is what you want?" "Yes, I'm positive"

As they hung up the phone Chey couldn't believe that she was about to put Tyrell in jail. Her rage was still stronger than her love for him, so a part of her didn't care. Her love for Angela was stronger than anything else, and she felt not only she was abandoned but so was her daughter.

As her thoughts started to wander, she gazed in the mirror and realized this was her life now. She adored Angela, but it was too difficult for her. She persuaded herself every day that she would be happy again and have the family she desires.

"Hello," Chey answered her phone.

"Girl comes downstairs, we are outside tonight. We are going to get some food and then head to a lounge. We both are going through hard times. We are going to make the best of this trip," Toya was yelling through the phone.

"Yeah you right let me get it together. I want to take some cute pictures anyway. I'll be down in twenty minutes."

"Twenty minutes!" Toya shouted louder. "Yes girl."

"Hurry up!" Toya said as she hung up the phone.

She didn't want to go out, but she needed to get everything off her mind. She quickly showered and changed into her black Alexander Wang dress and Bottega white heels. She quickly applied her eyelashes and concealer and dashed out the door.

⚹══════◄◆►══════⚹

TO BE CONTINUED.....

Stay tuned for series # 2: September 2022

Instagram: Timaaaaa_s

Made in United States
North Haven, CT
23 July 2022

21695540R00046